There's a Mouse in My House

ISBN 978-1-64114-222-9 (paperback)
ISBN 978-1-64114-223-6 (digital)

Copyright © 2018 by Judy Myers

Christian Faith Publishing, Inc.
832 Park Avenue
Meadville, PA 16335
www.christianfaithpublishing.com

Printed in the United States of America

There's a Mouse in My House

JUDY MYERS

There's a mouse in my house. I think he's planning to stay. He even took a shower with me today. He washed his hair, without a care, then ran away under the stair. I think he got very hungry. I found him by my fridge, but he got caught in a coil. Maybe he thought he'd try to act royal. He invited two friends, who were true to the end. Now they are sharing a meal.

"Come, let us run," said the little one and he happily let out a squeal! "Now we can play all night and day" was all that little one could say.

He ran around, not making a sound, hoping he wouldn't get caught. He tried to remember all that his mother had taught him to do. When he went out to play, he paused a moment, knelt on his knees, and started to pray. Then he ran back to find his friends, but they were nowhere to be found.

He called their name, but nobody came. So he began searching around. Then he heard a snap. Finding his friend on the other side in the trap, he started to cry.

"Dear Lord, hear my prayers, please don't let my little friend die."

All of a sudden his little friend broke free.

And he cried out, "Thank you, Lord, for hearing my plea."

The two walked away, beginning to pray, thanking the Lord up above. They ran in the sun, having some fun, feeling the warmth of each other's love.

Then they rested in a field, not wanting to yield to the cat that lived down the lane. They scampered along, singing a song, until they came upon an old broken drain.

Then they hid inside, and the little one cried, "I want to go home, can't you see."

His friend dried his teary eyes, saying, "Look up to the skies. On the stars you must make a wish."

As he started to look, they came to a brook that was filled with so many fish. Then he closed his eyes and paused for a bit, making a secret wish.

His friend gave a command, "Now take my hand. I'll lead you to some place that is warm. Hurry along, it's starting to rain, and we must get out of this storm."

Then they ran through a forest so creepy and dark and came upon a meadowlark who was digging for food in the ground. When she found some slugs, spiders and crickets, she began dancing around.

"I won't hurt you," she said to the mice. "I'm glad to have company. I think that it's nice."

The little one said, "I am hungry. Where can I find something to eat?"

The meadowlark said, "Come follow me, and I will lead you to a treat."

She led them down a trail, right to a garden wall. They climbed up oh so slowly so they wouldn't fall.

He just couldn't believe what he saw when he got to the other side. There were all kinds of fruits, veggies, and seeds. He closed his eyes, saying, "Lord, I knew that you would provide me with the things I daily need. To in this life begin to succeed."

After they had eaten their fill, they just lay down very still. They were tired from such a busy day. Then they heard a click-clank coming over a bank. They looked at each other with nothing to say.

When the sound got closer, they realized it was their friend, who was dragging a trap. They were relieved he was safe and sound, and he just needed a nap. As they surrounded him and started to pull the trap off, their chubby friend began to cough. He fell to his knees and let out a sneeze, but the trap was very stuck. His friends tried once more, tugging and pulling like before, but they had no luck. He then fell asleep, not making a peep, for he had such a hard day.

"What can we do, Lord, to help our friend," is all that they could say.

They all gathered around, not making a sound, trying to think of a plan. They talked all night, and to their delight an idea popped into their heads. They ran in the dark to their friend the meadowlark, asking him for his advice.

He let out a sound, to all around, hoping his song would sound nice. Then all of a sudden a large flock appeared. And all the mice scampered, trembling in fear. As the flock circled the mouse in the trap, they created a wind. The trap flew open with such a force it blew the mouse onto a fish's fin. The fish swam away with the mouse on his back into the deep blue sea.

The mouse then yelled very loud, "Oh, what's gonna happen to me?"

When the fish swam home, he said to his mom, "I've invited a friend."

His mom then explained how his friend couldn't live long in the sea.

"Okay, Mommy," the fish replied, "I will set him free." Then the fish swam and swam with the mouse on his back until he heard above him a duck go quack.

"Can you please help me out, I cannot go ashore," he said with a shout.

"Of course," said the duck. "Swim as close as you can. I will then help your little friend to reach dry land."

When the fish reached the duck, the mouse jumped up high.

"I made it," he said as he let out a cry. "Thank you, my friend, for carrying me. It was fun to travel along the sea."

Then the duck swam to land to let the mouse off his back. He wished him good luck and swam away with a quack.

"Oh dear," said the mouse. "What do I do now? I'm so far away, and I don't know how to get back to my friends. I wish I had a map." He sat, and he thought, *Oh, I guess I'll just take a nap.*

And when he awoke, it started to snow. He looked to the sky, saying, "Lord, which way I should go?"

Then he heard a voice from behind a tree. "Why don't you come home with me?"

When he looked, he saw a baby raccoon, who said to him, "It will be getting deep soon. My name is Bobby. I live in a den. I live with my friend, Roberta the wren. We share our den with Teddy the skunk. He sleeps downstairs on the top bunk. Then there's Suzy the owl, who is up all night. Her loud noises keep our enemies out of sight. You're more than welcome to come and stay, until this storm goes away."

Then Bobby and mouse ran through the snow right to the den that had a warm glow. Roberta had started the fireplace. Their den was so warm, and it had lots of space.

"You must be hungry," Roberta said. "I have just finished making chestnut pie. Come and sit down. I'll cut you a slice."

Then Bobby and mouse said, "That would be nice."

As they sat eating, Teddy came up the stairs. "Something smells good. No one can compare to Roberta's cooking. She keeps us well fed. She reads us a story and tucks us in bed."

Roberta just smiled as she sat down to eat. "You all are so kind. Oh, what a treat it is to serve you, my little ones. I thank the Lord when each day is done."

As they all finished eating, they cleared their plates.

Roberta looked at the clock and said, "Oh my, it is late! Time for you little ones to get into bed. Go to the bathroom, wash your hands and face, brush your teeth, put a cap on the toothpaste. Climb under the covers. I'll tuck you in, close your little eyes, and begin to think of the good things that happened today. Finally, thank God when you pray." She gave them a kiss, turned off the light, closed the door, and said good night. Roberta then climbed the stairs and said her prayers. She finished straightening the house and checked on the little mouse. Then she went to bed and fell right to sleep.

When morning came, she heard a little peep. She looked and looked all around. There was the mouse with tears in his eyes. "Come, little one, why is it you cry?" Then she lifted him up upon her knee.

"I had a bad dream. A cat was chasing me."

Roberta then gave him a hug. "No cat will come here. You are snug as a bug. Now it is early. You must go back to bed."

"Will you tuck me in?" the little mouse said.

"Of course, I will" Roberta replied. "Now come, little one, let's dry your eye. Nothing will happen. You are safe. Please don't cry. Suzy the owl keeps watch all night long. Ask God to make you brave, ask him to make you strong."

Then little mouse hugged Roberta, and she tucked him in bed. "Thank you, Roberta," was what he said. She sang him a song. He went fast to sleep. She said a prayer that the Lord would keep this little mouse in his tender care, showing him that he's always there.

When they awoke, the ground was covered in snow, the sun shining down its radiant glow.

"I'm hungry," said Teddy. "Is it time to eat? I smell something good. I smell something sweet."

They came to the table, and they said their prayers. Roberta made cereal, biscuits, and pears.

"It all looks so yummy," said the little mouse. "I thank you for welcoming me to your house."

Bobby came running up the stairs. "My favorite, biscuits and pears. Please pass the sugar," he said as he sat. "Please pass the butter. I just need a pat."

"Don't forget, Bobby, to say a prayer, tuck in your napkin, and pull in your chair."

Then Bobby lowered his head and folded his paws. And in his prayer he said, "Thank you, dear Lord, for this yummy meal, for the hands who prepared it." Then he let out a squeal.

He ate all his breakfast, put his dish in the sink, ran back down the stairs, and began to think of all the great things he shared with his friends.

"I pray this time, Lord, never ends." He made his bed, and then he got dressed and reflected upon how he'd been blessed.

Then Teddy came running down the stairs. He too made his bed, and then said his prayers.

"I thank you, dear Lord, for sending little mouse. It's fun having him here in our house. He loves to play games. He is fun to be around. Thank you for the new friend we've found."

Then Roberta shouted, "What's taking you all so long to get ready? Come along, little ones, that includes you, Teddy."

"Where are we going?" was Teddy's reply.

"We must find some berries to make a pie."

They all scampered out into the snow, but they couldn't find which way to go. The path that they traveled was all gone now.

"What do we do? We don't have a plow."

They all went back to the tree, took off their boots, and played monopoly. They all had such fun as they rounded the board

"I'm buying a house," said Bobby. "I'm now a landlord."

Little mouse threw the dice. "Look, I got doubles, not once, but twice." He then moved his piece, landing in jail. "Oh dear," said the mouse. "I don't have the bail."

"That's all right, little mouse," was Bobby's reply. "All you must do is throw the die. If you get doubles, one more time it gets you out of jail for the crime you did. Don't do it again."

The little mouse squealed, then shouted, "Amen."

"Who's hungry for lunch? Finish your game. It's almost noon. Go to the drawer, get your fork and your spoon. Take them to the table. It's time to eat." Roberta then yelled, "I have such a treat. We have berries and nuts. We have cake, pie, and ice cream."

Bobby, Teddy, and mouse thought that it was a dream.

They sat in their chairs, and they said their prayers. They began to eat their wonderful treat.

"Thank you, Roberta. That was so yummy. Now we are full in our tummy."

Then they all cleared the plates, placing them in the sink.

"What shall we do now? Let's sit and think."

They sat on the couch, and they read some books. They looked out the window, and just by the brook were three little deer and a mama deer too. They were searching for food.

Mama said, "What will we do?"

Then Roberta called to them to come in and eat. "I will fix you some berries and nuts for a treat."

The deer then came into their home.

Mama said, "I didn't think we would roam this far away from our home. My name is Cindy. My girls are Debbie, Sandy, and Gail. We have wandered too far from the trail. I thank you for your hospitality. It was starting to get cold for the girls and me."

"How about some tea?" Roberta asked.

Debbie, Sandy, and Gail said, "This place is a blast!"

"Come play with us," said Bobby, Teddy, and mouse. "It is so much fun to live in this house."

Cindy and Roberta watched the little ones play.

Debbie ran to her mama. "Can we stay? Can we stay?"

"I don't want to impose upon this kind family."

Roberta replied, "Stay as long as you like. Please feel free. Our home is yours as long as you'd like to stay."

Then the girls jumped up and down. "Come, let us pray. Thank you, dear Lord, for meeting our needs, for this little wren who will feed us with love and her constant care. But most of all, thank you, Lord, for being there." Then the girls ran to play with Bobby and Teddy.

"You're it, Debbie, go count. We are ready. So close your eyes, and don't you dare peek."

They all ran to hide. Sandy hid in the cupboard till she heard the little mouse cry.

"Why are you crying?" she shouted.

Then little mouse showed her his tail and began to pout.

"Come, little one," said Roberta the wren. "I'll make it all better again." She went to the bathroom to get out the first aid kit. "Don't worry, dear, this won't hurt a bit." She wrapped up his tail with a little gauze. "Now run and play. Don't touch your tail with your paws. We must keep it clean so it can heal."

"Thank you, Roberta," he said with a squeal. He ran to play with Debbie, Sandy, and Gail. And soon he forgot all about his tail.

After fixing mouse's tail, Roberta sat down again to get acquainted with her new friend. They learned all about each other's family. Then all of a sudden there was a loud crash. Teddy, while running, knocked over the trash.

"What is going on?" yelled Roberta. "What was that noise?"

Cindy then said, "Boys will be boys!"

Roberta and Cindy then swept the floor. They both yelled, "Stop it, no more running."

"It's time to settle down. Let's find a movie," Cindy said with a frown. "I will not have you children making a riot. Now it is time to sit still and be quiet."

They all sat on pillows across the floor.

Then Cindy said, "Girls, remember, no more!"

They all sat quietly watching TV.

"I knew they could do it, but I had to see. Now what were we talking about before all the commotion? You were telling me how you wish you had some potion that would give you the energy you need each day," Roberta said.

Cindy said to Roberta, "Let's agree and pray."

Cindy started first. "Lord, give us the wisdom to guide all the children we love. Give us your compassion sent down from above."

Roberta continued, "May we have the strength and endurance to lead the way our little ones must go each day."

They both said "Amen" and gave each other a hug. They went to the kitchen and refilled their mug. When they finished their tea, they heard a knock on the door.

Cindy said, "Who can this be?" as she walked across the floor.

"Be careful," shouted Roberta. "You just don't know who it can be. I'm not expecting company."

They looked out the window to see who was there. It turned out to be Benny the bear.

"I just couldn't sleep. How my daddy does snore. I couldn't take the noise anymore. I brought some honey and homemade jam." He closed the door with a very big slam.

"Please be more careful with my door," Roberta said.

Benny turned around and bumped his head.

Roberta rubbed his head with the top of her hand, then turned to him and gave a command.

"Why not join the others? They're watching TV. We just bought a new movie. Go, look, and see."

Benny sat with the others upon the floor.

Roberta then whispered, "There's always room for one more."

Benny sat eating popcorn and drinking some pop. He wished that this party would never stop.

Then all of a sudden a knock came on the door.

Cindy looked at Roberta, saying, "There's always room for one more."

They both walked very quickly and looked through the keyhole.

"Who's out there?" they shouted.

"It's Betsy the mole. I can't see that well," said Betsy to Cindy. "My home has been ruined, and I can't find my sister Mindy. She went for a walk before the snow started. She's never been away from home. We've never been parted. She's very fragile. She gets nervous when she's alone. I've noticed that she forgot her phone. I hope and I pray that she is all right. I have been searching all through the night. You know it's hard, this searching, for me. It's very difficult when you can't see."

"I can help you look," a voice shouted from downstairs. "I'll pack my backpack. You know it's easier in pairs." Walking upstairs came Teddy the skunk. His backpack on his back, he was such a cool punk. "Let's go," he said to Betsy the mole. "I bet we find Mindy hiding in a hole."

"I hope and pray that you are right. I find it hard sleeping at night. Without my sister, I cannot move. We help each other to improve the way we share in our daily chores. I just wish that I had locked the doors."

"It's not your fault your sister walked outside. I know she probably went for a ride on her new sled. Oh, how she loves the snow. I wonder which way that she would go. Why don't we check the trail leading to the cave? The path is narrow. We must be brave. Come on, Betsy. Come take my hand, and I will lead you through this land."

So up they climbed very carefully, hoping to see. They reached the top of the mountain range.

Betsy said, "Oh, I feel something strange. I can't explain the way that I feel, but my stomach's in knots, and I pray this will reveal where Mindy is, whether dead or alive. I'm hoping that she was strong enough to survive."

Then they walked through the cave, searching up and down. They heard a strange noise on the ground. They turned a corner. They walked through a tunnel. Then they strolled up a pathway and found Mindy lying there. Is she all right? Is she dead?

Betsy had terrible thoughts in her head. She knelt by her sister, who was lying very still, then said a prayer, "Lord, whatever is in your will." Betsy shook and shook Mindy, but her sister wouldn't wake up. She found a pool of water. Using a rock for a cup, she tried to make Mindy drink as she bent her head.

Teddy sorrowfully said, "I think that she is dead. I'm sorry, Betsy." Teddy cried.

Betsy said, "Oh, why had she lied. She shouldn't have gone sledding alone, especially without her phone."

Then they made a cot out of sticks, leaves, and twine. They walked down the mountain in a straight line. When they reached their final destiny, they laid Mindy, in a small grave. Then they bowed their heads saying a prayer, "Oh my, she was awful brave."

24

They walked in the house hand in hand. Their faces had said it all.

"You two must be tired," Roberta called.

Betsy ran into Roberta's arms, and she cried and cried.

"You both did your best," Roberta said.

Cindy chimed in, "You're both really tired." Cindy made tea.

They sat at the table and quietly said a prayer.

Then Betsy said, "I should have gone with Mindy. I should have been there."

"You can't blame yourself for what others do. You must ask the Lord to see you through. He will give you the strength and the courage to go on. You must believe you'll see a new dawn."

Then Betsy went downstairs to get some rest. She knew she'd feel better after a nap. She showered, and then she fell asleep upon Cindy's lap. Cindy cuddled her in her arms of love. Then she prayed that God would guide her from heaven above. Then Cindy placed her upon an empty bed. She covered her up and kissed her head. She climbed the stairs and saw Teddy crying. She lifted him up, saying, "Thank you for trying. You are so brave for helping."

Teddy said with a frown, "All I feel like is yelping. It was hard to see Mindy dead on the ground. I tried to be brave when we found her lying there. I said a prayer, asking God, 'Why?' But all I could do is cry."

Roberta then walked in the room, patting Teddy upon the back. "I know this is hard for you to take. Why don't you come and have some cake."

He sat down. They talked. Then she rubbed his back, saying, "Remember, with Jesus there is no lack. Mindy's in heaven, dancing on clouds, no longer sad, feeling so proud. Mindy is happy though we are sad. Betsy must remember all the good times they had. It may take a long time for her sadness to end. She will need you, Teddy, to be a good friend. Now go get some rest, my dear little one. You make me feel proud that you are my son."

"Aw shucks," said Teddy as he dried his eye.

Roberta then said, "Little one, don't you cry. Come on, Teddy, let's get you some rest. Go take your shower and then get dressed in your pajamas. I'll tuck you in tight. You have been out, searching all night."

Teddy did what Roberta said. Then she tucked him in tight and kissed his head. It didn't take long for him to go to sleep. Before Roberta left his room, she prayed the Lord would keep him safe and warm with a compassionate heart. Then she prayed that the Lord would start to heal and to make them both feel strong and that it wouldn't take very long.

She walked upstairs, saying, "What can we feed this bunch?"

Cindy called Debbie, Sandy, and Gail. "Run to the cupboard. Go, get a pail. Then go in the forest get me berries, nuts, and twigs. We'll make a feast of what we can dig. Out of the pantry, we'll have a big party. We have honey and grains. We will eat very hardy."

They grabbed their pails and trotted along singing one of their favorite songs.

They reached a bush with berries and started placing them in their pail. They filled it up to the top as they walked leaving a trail.

"Hurry," said Sandy to Debbie and Gail. "I think that we have a hole in our pail."

They moved very quickly. They reached the door, opened it up, and fell on the floor. But Cindy was quick. She caught the pail in the air, saving the berries from going everywhere.

"Good catch, Mom!" said Sandy. "I think that it was quite dandy!"

Then the girls went to see what Bobby was playing. He was reading a book about slaying, a dragon in a Nintendo game, but he forgot the dragon's name.

The little mouse said, "Isn't his name Nate? The name of the book you are reading is *Nate the Great.* It's about a dragon who lives with his grandmother. She helps him to take care of his little brother. Nate works very hard and gets good grades in school. His little brother thinks Nate is so cool. When Nate's not in school, he goes walking in the woods. He hunts for so many interesting goods. One day he found a snake stuck under a rock. He picked up the rock, and to his shock, the snake was still quiet alive. He was surprised it did survive. Then he continued on his walk through the woods, collecting more of nature's goods. He found a trail leading to a cave. He decided to explore. He decided to be brave. So he entered the cave, and to his surprise, staring at him were one hundred eyes. He realized he found a home of bats. Looking down on the ground, he found their friends the rats. At first he was scared, and he wanted to run. But the bats said to him, 'Come and have some fun. We will not harm you. We like having company.' Then the rats chimed in, 'You're just in time for tea.' Nate couldn't believe all that was hearing. He sat on a rock, and his new friends started cheering. Then they had tea and got to know each other. Nate said to his friend, 'You must meet my brother. I must leave now. My grandmother will worry. I've been gone all day. I must scurry.' So Nate waved good-bye and went on his way. He just made it home in time to pray, for dinner was almost done. And he wanted to tell everyone of the fun." Little mouse then finished his story and said, "You must read the book for yourself."

"That was very good timing," Roberta said. "I've just finished baking the bread. Cindy made berry jam. All I need is to wait for the ham. It's almost ready. Go wake Betsy and Teddy and tell them that dinner will soon be ready."

So Bobby and Gail held on to the rail as they went to wake Betsy and Ted. They said, "Get up, sleepyheads, time to get out of your beds."

Roberta and Cindy have dinner all done, so they all went upstairs, quickly going to their chairs.

Roberta said, "Little ones, we must not run. Betsy and Teddy, how do you feel?"

"We are so hungry we could eat this whole meal. We're still a bit sad," said Betsy and Ted.

Roberta smiled. "You will feel better once you are fed."

I'm not very hungry," Betsy replied. "I miss my sister. Why did she die?"

Then Cindy came into the room with shepherd's pie.

Roberta said, "Come, little one, we must talk. Let's go to the living room. Let's take a walk."

While Cindy fed the rest of the crew, Roberta took Betsy. She knew what she must do.

They sat on the couch, Betsy started to cry. She said, "I don't understand. I don't know why?"

Roberta said, "A lot of things happen we don't understand. Our future is placed in God's hands. Maybe he needed Mindy for a special deed. She was the only one who could succeed. She is walking with Jesus upon golden streets. Her life on earth has been complete. She knows that you miss her. She's watching you from above. And when you see a rainbow shine, she's sending you her love." Roberta then said, "Now, little one, do you understand? Come, dry your tears. Come, take my hand. It will get better as the days go by, for when you see that rainbow, you will no longer cry. You will smile to heaven above, knowing that Mindy sends you her love."

Then Betsy said, "Thank you, I think I now understand."

They walked back to the table hand in hand.

"Come sit next to me," Teddy replied.

Then Betsy smiled and dried her eye. Betsy reached for the bread and the homemade jam, then took a slice of the ham. "Please, pass the mustard," she asked with a grin. "I think I already begin to feel better knowing Mindy's watching me. Cindy, please pour me a cup of tea."

Cindy went to the stove and turned off the kettle. She smiled at Betsy, saying, "I believe this will settle your upset tummy. Please drink your tea slowly, you'll feel better soon. There's a honey in the cupboard, I'll get you a spoon."

Betsy drank all her tea and placed her cup in the sink. Then she went downstairs to think. She sat on her bed, meditating upon all she had been through, thinking, *What's going on? I'm thankful for finding a new family. Before it was only Mindy and me. Teddy's so sweet. He's always by my side. Bobby and little mouse love to play and hide. Then there's Debbie and Gail and Sandy too. They are so loving in all they do. Roberta makes me feel special like I was her own. Cindy makes sure that I'm not alone. Although I miss Mindy, she's in a better place. I thank you, dear Lord, for showing me your grace.*

When Betsy was done saying her prayers, she ran up the stairs. She helped Cindy clear the table and push in the chairs.

After they both were all done, Roberta came in, saying, "Let's have some fun." She formed two teams for a relay race. "Okay, everybody, go to your place. The first team to get ducks lined up will win this magic golden cup."

Cindy then cheered, "Come on, Debbie, Sandy, and Gail. You must move faster and not leave a trail of ducks all over the floor. Get them in a row. Come on, let's score!"

The next team in line was Teddy, Betsy, and Bobby.

"Come on," yelled Roberta. "This was your hobby. You can do it, you three. Now line them up in a row. You just have one more to go."

The race continued. It ended in a tie.

"You all did very well," Roberta did cry. "Now let's have some quiet time. You may play a game, rest, or read. While Cindy and I figure out what to feed you all for dinner, let's see what we can find. There's soup, bread, and honey we can combine to make you a yummy little treat. Now go wash your hands, it's almost time to eat."

Roberta then made some toast and honey while Cindy prepared some soup that smelled funny.

Cindy said, "I checked the label. It's way before the expiration date. I even gave it a taste, so don't hesitate to eat this soup. There is nothing wrong it says on the label. It will build strong muscles and give you extra energy. Maybe it should just be for Roberta and me."

Then everyone laughed as they sat down and passed the food all around.

After their meal was done, Teddy said, "Let's go out and run. The snow is melting on the ground I can see green grass all around."

Roberta said, "It's been a long winter. I'm so glad it's over. Look out the window, I think I see a clover. Is it four leafed? You know that's good luck."

Cindy said, "Please help me open this window. It is very stuck."

Roberta walked over and gave it a tug. Up went the window, and on the sill was a dead bug. Then Roberta grabbed a rag and some bleach, started cleaning the window, but the top was too hard to reach. She then swept the floor and mopped it too. There seemed to be so much she had to do.

The sun shone down brightly. Its warmth felt so good. Cindy knew she and the girls would soon go back into the woods. She felt so blessed to have found a new friend and hoped that this friendship would never end.

They both finished dusting and sweeping. They sat at the table and started weeping.

"The winter's been special when we all came together. We've been through all types of stormy weather."

They both sat at the table, waiting for the coffee to brew. Cindy stood and got cups, knowing what she must do. She then called for Debbie, Sandy, and Gail. She said, "Girls, we must soon find that trail that leads to our home I know you don't want to go. We only promised to stay till after the snow. It's all melted now. We must be on our way, but before we go, let's take this time to pray."

So they all gathered round in a circle, holding hands with tears in their eyes, thinking of all the grand times that they shared in this spacious tree. Then the prayer started with Cindy. She thanked the Lord for showing her and her girls grace and helping them find such an awesome place. Then Debbie continued with thanking God for her new friends. Sandy chimed in, "Who were true to the end." Then Gail wiped the tears streaming down her face, saying, "Thank you, dear Lord, for all of your grace."

Roberta then ended, "You silly girls, you know, you really don't have to go."

Cindy smiled. "Our family is probably looking for us. We must rebuild our home. We must!"

They gathered their things and sadly walked out the door. Sandy, Cindy, Debbie, and Gail had much to explore. They all waved good-bye. As they went along, soon Debbie and Sandy were singing a song.

Gail looked at Cindy with tears in her eyes. "Mama, why is it always hard saying good-byes."

As they trotted along, Cindy explained, "Good-byes aren't forever. In our hearts they will remain."

Roberta waved to Cindy and her family. She had tears in her eyes, saying, "I'll miss their company." Then she went on cleaning till the tree house did shine. She knew it was almost time to dine. She called out to Teddy, Bobby, and mouse, "It's time for dinner. Wipe your feet before walking into this house."

They all sat down to a wondrous meal.

"Where's Betsy?" said little mouse as he let out a squeal.

"I'm right here," was Betsy's reply

"Come to the table. We're having vegetable pie."

"That's one of my favorites in the world."

Then they all bowed in silence, thanking God for his love unfurled.

Roberta then smiled as she cut each one a slice. "You've all been so helpful. I think it's so nice."

They all ate in silence, enjoying each bite.

Then Betsy announced, "I'm leaving tonight. I thank you, Roberta, for your loving care and to Teddy and Bobby for always being there and to little mouse for your friendship and love and to Mindy, who is watching me from above."

"You don't have to leave," was Roberta's reply. "You're part of our family." A tear dropped from her eye.

"I'll miss you," said Teddy. "Please don't go away."

Then Bobby chimed in, "Why don't we just pray."

So they all gathered in a circle of love. Thanking the Lord in heaven above, asking him to guide Betsy along her way and protect her each and every day. Then Betsy chimed in, asking the Lord to send down His blessing and to reward Roberta, Bobby, and Teddy for their gift of concern. And she thanked the Lord for all she had learned from this gracious mother and her two sons for helping her out when the day is done.

Then little mouse said, "Betsy, I will miss you and all of the fun things we used to do."

Roberta then prayed, "Dear Lord, guide and protect this little one. Give her your strength when this day is done. To go forward in whatever your will is for her. Over these months, she has begun to mature. Help her find shelter, help her find love, and rain down upon her your blessings from above."

Then everyone said a loud "Amen!"

Teddy chimed in, "You better come and visit again."

"I will," promised Betsy.

As she walked out the door, Roberta said, "Remember, we've always room for one more."

They all stood by the door as Betsy walked up the hill. They waved, and they shouted and then closed the door. With everyone gone, the house was so still.

Then all of a sudden there was a knock on the door.

Roberta whispered, "There's always room for one more."

She opened the door, and to her surprise, there stood two little mice with tears in their eyes.

"We've lost our friend when it began to snow. Now we don't know which way to go."

Then the little mouse ran into their arms. "Thank you, Lord, they were not harmed. I'm so glad to see you, my little friends. I prayed each night that we would make amends. And now you are standing in front of me. I can hardly believe what I see."

"Will you come home with us, little mouse. It's lonely without you in the house."

"I'd love to," said little mouse with a smile on his face. "Come let us retrace the pathway we took. It won't take too long. I know you will make it. I know you are strong." Then little mouse waved as he walked through the door. "Thank you, Roberta, now it's time to explore."

Roberta then waved with Teddy and Bobby by her side. Then she shouted, "Remember, the Lord will provide."

Little mouse waved as he scampered along. They all were so happy, they started singing a song.

"What a busy winter we've had," Roberta then said. "Now who is hungry for some jam and bread?"

Teddy raised his hand. Bobby did too. They sat at the table, talking of all they've been through.

The springtime had come. The snow was all gone. It was a new day! It was a new dawn! They would once again be a family of three. They would all gather berries from that big tree in the middle of the forest. They would live happily!

About the Author

Judy loves writing. Her stories seem to reflect the experiences that happened in her life. She enjoys being with children. She has been striving to tell her story in ways that can be understood by children. Her story is a teaching story. It teaches children compassion and learning to get lessons from life's experiences.

CPSIA information can be obtained
at www.ICGtesting.com
Printed in the USA
BVHW020037111019
560836BV00001B/4/P

9 781641 14222